nickelodeon

SPONGEBOB SQUAREPANTS™

SPONGE
AT HEART

How to Live a Bikini Bottom Life

By Melissa Wygand

Random House 🏠 New York

created by

Stephen Hillenburg

ISBN 978-1-9848-9409-0

Printed in the United States of America

10 9 8 7 6 5 4 3 2 1

Life

Today is the first day
of the rest of your life.

Remember to make time for hobbies
outside of work or school.

Don't be afraid to
stand up for yourself.

"*Excuse me, sir—you're sitting on my body, which is also my face.*"

Practice makes perfect . . .
most of the time.

The most important things
in life can't be bought.

Or can they?

If you want to remember
something, write it down.

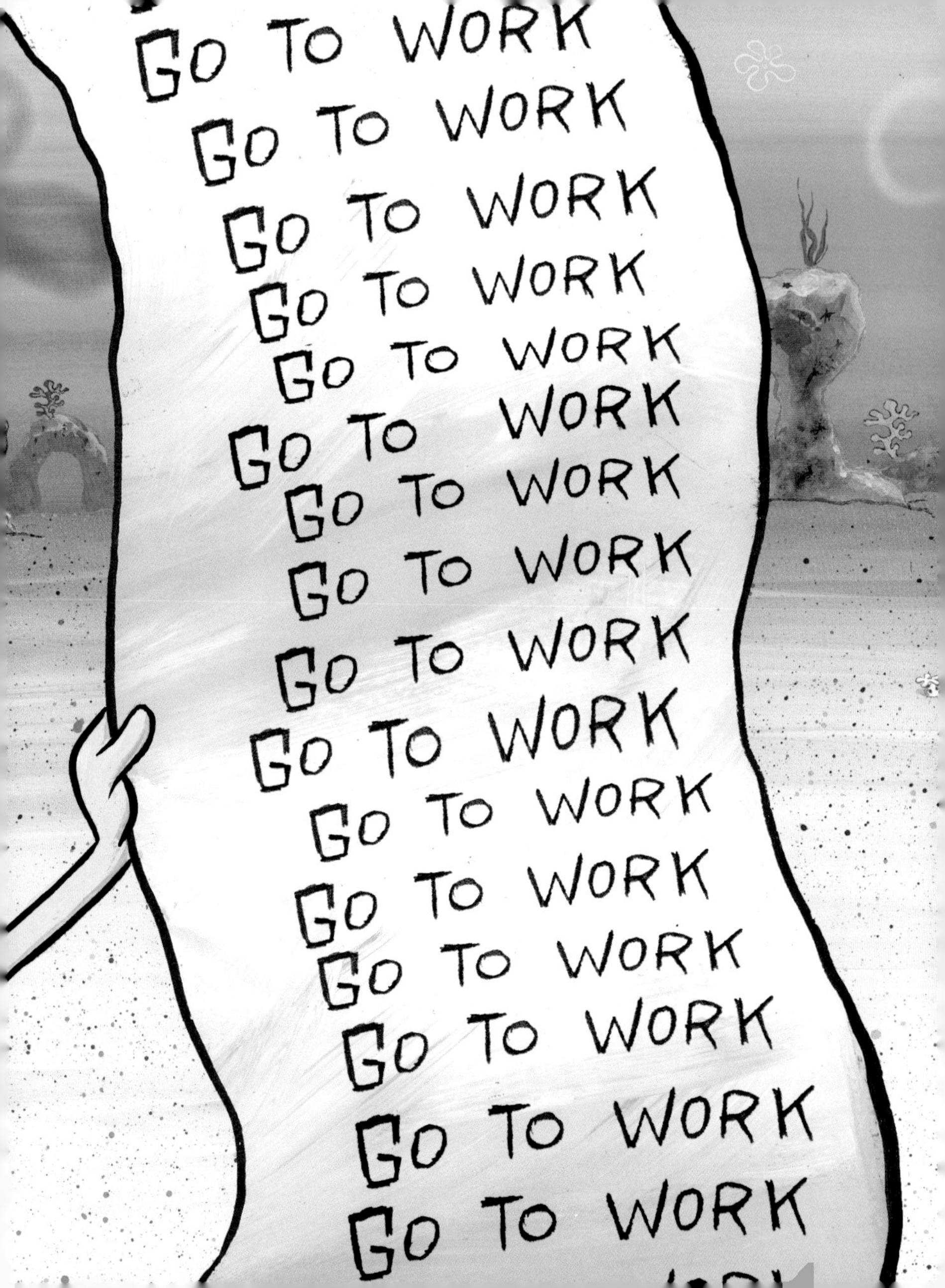
GO TO WORK
GO TO WORK
GO TO WORK
GO TO WORK
GO TO WORK
GO TO WORK
GO TO WORK
GO TO WORK
GO TO WORK
GO TO WORK
GO TO WORK
GO TO WORK
GO TO WORK
GO TO WORK
GO TO WORK
GO TO WORK

Don't underestimate the
power of a good night's sleep.

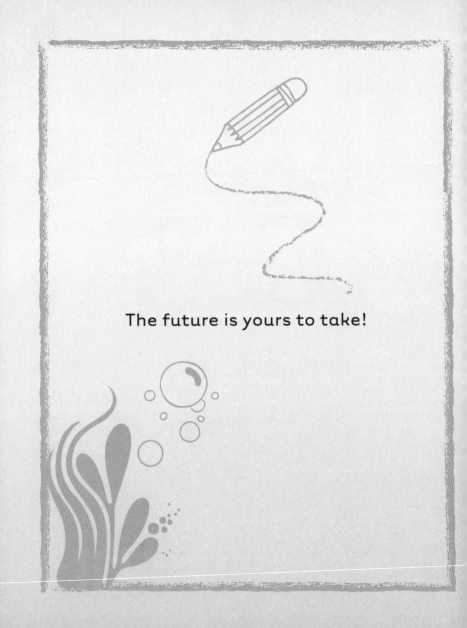

The future is yours to take!

"Me hoy minoy!"

FRIDAY NIGHTS

EXPECTATION

AS AN ADULT

REALITY

Relationships

You never forget your first love.

No one ever said dating is easy.
And if they did, they're lying.

The best kinds of gifts
are from the heart.

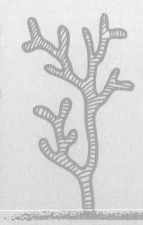

*"I couldn't afford a present
this year, so I got you this box."*

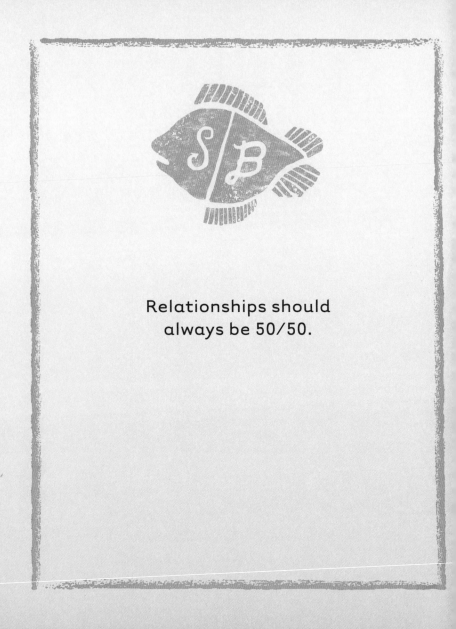

Relationships should
always be 50/50.

Communication is the key
to a successful marriage.

"Sheldon, honey, in order to steal the Krabby Patty form—"

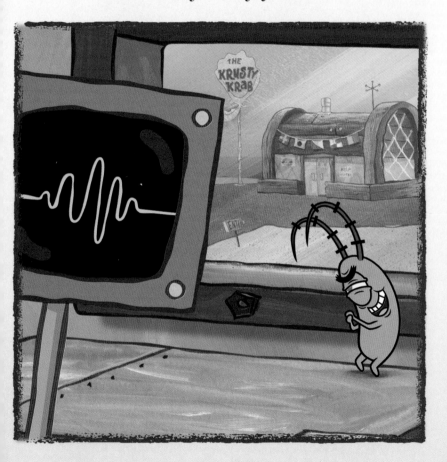

"Hush, Karen—I'm thinking of ways to steal the Krabby Patty formula!"

Always let your partner know
how much you care about them.

Work

Find a job you're passionate about
and it won't feel like work.

If at first you don't succeed, try again.
And again. And again. And again . . .

Good coworkers can become
some of your best friends.

Treat your employees with respect
and don't micromanage their time.

Take breaks throughout the day
when needed so you can focus.

Keep your cool, even with
the most difficult customers.

Health &
Fitness

Take care of your body
by eating healthy foods.

Not a master chef? Learn how to make a few simple meals and you'll be set.

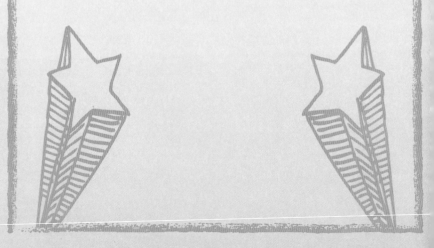

*"Holographic meatloaf—
my favorite!"*

Never skip leg day.

Challenge yourself to go
a little further each day.

Fashion & Trends

"Is life totally unfair for the third time this week?

Sounds like someone needs a shopping trip!"

Keep your fashion game on point.

How to Be Fancy

1. Take frequent bubble baths.

2. Keep art all around your house, especially self-portraits.

3. Eat tetrazzini.

4. Binge-watch House Fancy.

5. Listen to smooth jazz, particularly Kelpy G.

"Table for one, please."

Hairdresser:
What do you want me to do?

Me:
Just a trim, thanks.

Hairdresser:
No problem.

And always remember—
if you've got it, flaunt it!